# ANIMAZE !

## A Collection of Amazing Nature Mazes

by WENDY MADGWICK

illustrated by LORNA HUSSEY

RAGGED BEARS

*For my grandparents*
*Dan and Agnes Johnson — L.H.*
*For my family — W.M.*

First published in Great Britain in 1992
by Ragged Bears Limited,
Ragged Appleshaw,
Andover, Hampshire SP11 9HX.

Devised and produced by The Templar Company plc.,
Pippbrook Mill, London Road, Dorking, Surrey RH4 1JE.

Designed by Janie Louise Hunt
Colour separations by Positive Colour Ltd.,
Maldon, Essex

Printed in Italy

ISBN 1 85714 015 X

# Finding the way

A little zebra is lost in the grasslands. He's trying to reach his mother, but cheetahs are lurking nearby, and a hungry lioness is on the prowl.

You can help by finding the right path through the grassland maze and the other nature mazes in this book. Each maze is set in a different habitat — from the icy Arctic to the tropical jungles of South America. Trace the correct path through the maze with your finger. Along the way you'll meet lots of other animals — strange little fish that climb trees and walk on mud, a desert cat that can knock birds out of midair, and more. But be careful — the wrong path could lead to trouble.

All the solutions are at the back of the book, where you'll also find "nature notes" that will tell you about the animals in each picture.

## SWAMPLANDS

    Silently the evening tide has swept into the mangrove swamps that surround Borneo, an island in South East Asia. Startled, a male proboscis monkey looks up as he hears the call of the other monkeys on the mainland. He has been exploring and is now stranded on a small island. The other monkeys are feeding along the shore and he wants to join in the feast. A strong swimmer, the monkey can weave his way through the water and get back to shore — but some paths are blocked by the tangled roots of the mangrove trees and the creatures that inhabit this strange world. Can you find the way back?

# A WORLD IN MINIATURE

In the gloom of a South American jungle, tiny leaf-cutter ants are cutting off pieces of leaf to take back to their underground nest. Then they scuttle along the forest floor, following well-worn scent trails that will lead them home. But they must be careful. Many of their trails are blocked by other animals. A sticky-tongued anteater is on the prowl, looking for a meal. Fierce-jawed soldier termites block another path, and a tiny antbird is pecking its way along another. Only one route leads home, but which one?
See if you can find the safe path back to the ants' nest.

# UPSTREAM

At long last the exhausted salmon have reached their journey's end. They have travelled hundreds of kilometres across the sea to return to the North American river in which they were born. Now they must make their way upstream to the spawning grounds, where the females will lay their eggs. The journey is beset by many hazards — rockfalls block the way, and bears and ospreys fish for their dinner as otters and beavers swim and play in the streams. Follow the maze of waterways and see if you can find the route to the salmon's spawning ground. Only one stream is safe, however. All the rest lead to disaster.

# DESERT WASTES

As the afternoon draws to a close and the shadows lengthen, the animals of the Sahara desert make their way toward the oasis for a much-needed drink of water and to feed on seeds and insects. Some animals are already there, lapping up the cool water. Other animals are on their way. Which animals reach the oasis safely? Follow the hoofprints of the camel and oryx, the pawprints of the fox and caracal, and the tiny marks left by the jerboa and gerbil as they hop across the plain. Which ones make it safely to the water hole?

# ON THE RIVER

The river is bathed in the warm, hazy sunshine of an early summer's day. Suddenly the peace is broken by a sharp sound. The male beaver lifts his head to listen. There it is again: "Slap! Slap! Slap!" His mate is slapping her large, flattened tail on the water to warn of danger. She will then dive beneath the water with their two babies and seek the safety of their lodge deep within the dam. The male beaver must swim home quickly. But there are many animals on the river, and he does not want to disturb them. Can you find the way back to the dam? Follow the maze of waterways, but be careful — only one route is clear of all other creatures.

# THE OUTBACK

The bark of a dingo as it calls to its pups echoes across the plains of the Australian outback. Startled, three little red kangaroos, called joeys, look up. They have become separated from their mothers. Frightened, they rush back to the safety of their mothers' pouches. But the way is not clear, they must avoid many objects. Mallee fowl are nesting, and two young emus scratch at the grassy scrubland near their father. Termite mounds tower over the landscape, and the fearless thorny devil and Gould's goanna scuttle into the shade to escape the heat of the sun. Which joey belongs to which mother? Follow the trails and see if you can find out.

# IN THE JUNGLE

High in the tree tops of a South American jungle, a troupe
of chattering squirrel monkeys and their young is travelling in
search of food. Far below they see the juicy, golden fruit of the
guava tree. But their way is blocked by many animals feeding and
sleeping in the heat of the day. They must not disturb the
toucans, macaws and tamarins, as their noisy calls will alert every
creature in the forest. They must creep past the prowling jaguar
and the menacing snakes that sometimes eat small monkeys —
and they must not wake the sleeping ocelot. Follow the maze
of large branches that lead to the fruit, but be careful —
it won't be easy; only one route is safe.

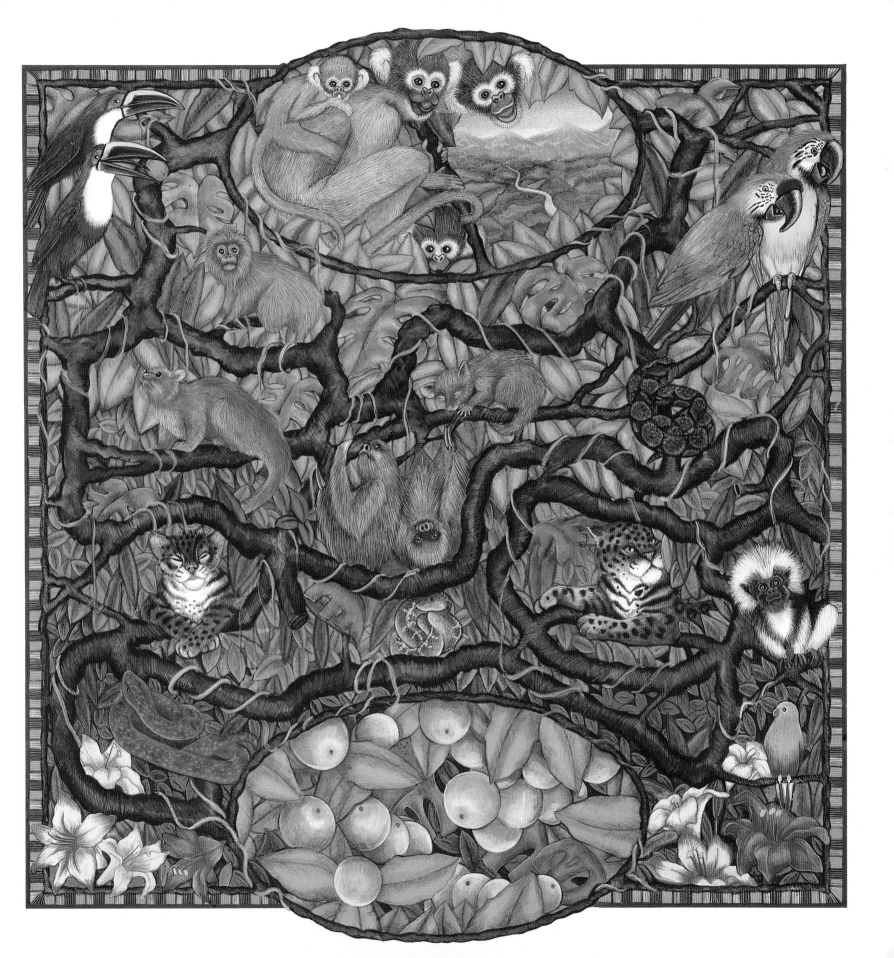

# AT THE WATER HOLE

Just after sunrise, before the baking sun rises high above the African savanna, or grasslands, many animals make their way to the water hole to drink. A young zebra has become separated from the herd as they travelled across the plains to quench their thirst. Wide-eyed, the foal looks out over the dusty grasslands. It can see the herd in the distance, but there are many dangers as well. Lions, cheetahs and other hungry predators hide, waiting to pounce on unsuspecting prey. Hippos wallow, long-necked giraffes nibble at leafy trees and wildebeest and deer graze. See if you can find the way to the water hole, but beware — only one path is clear.

# ON THE REEF

Teeming with life, Australia's Great Barrier Reef is like an underwater jungle. Thousands of beautiful sea creatures live among the ornate and colourful corals. Here, the banded angelfish has been out foraging for food, but as evening falls, it seeks its shelter deep within the coral reef, near other angelfish. The fish makes its way home, but its route is blocked by its enemies and by other creatures probing the crevices in search of food. Only one path is clear and will lead the angelfish safely home. Try to find it, but beware — the eagle ray, shark and octopus are waiting to pounce!

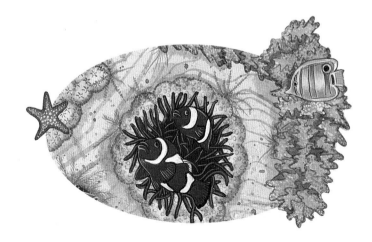

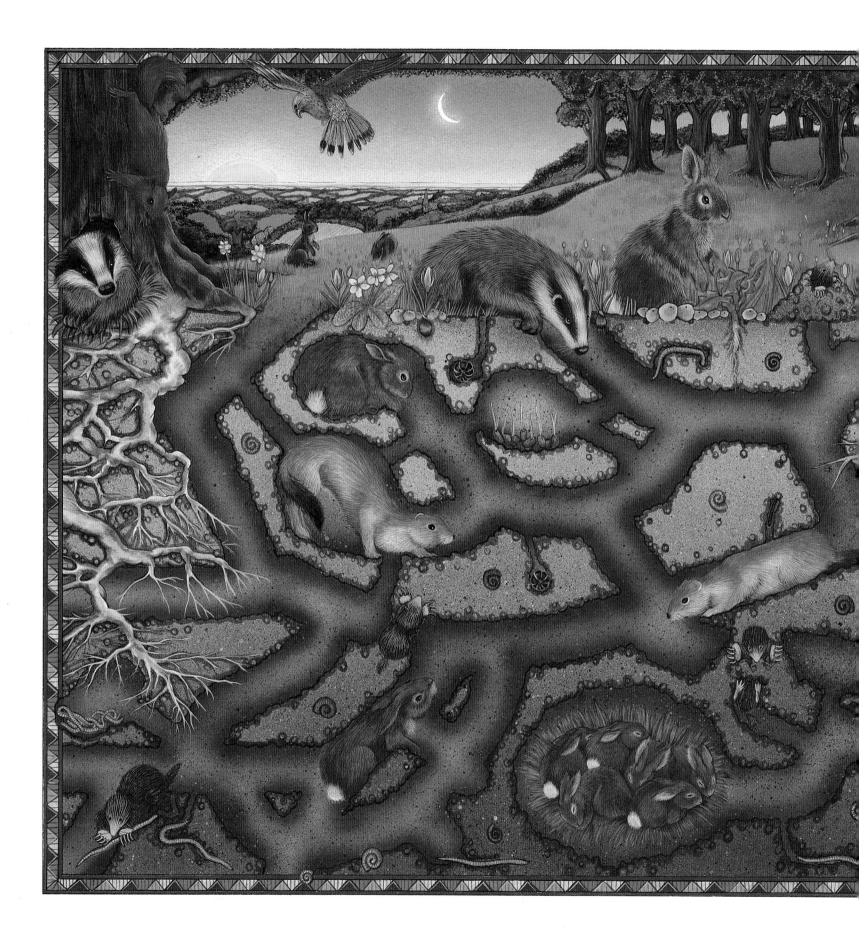

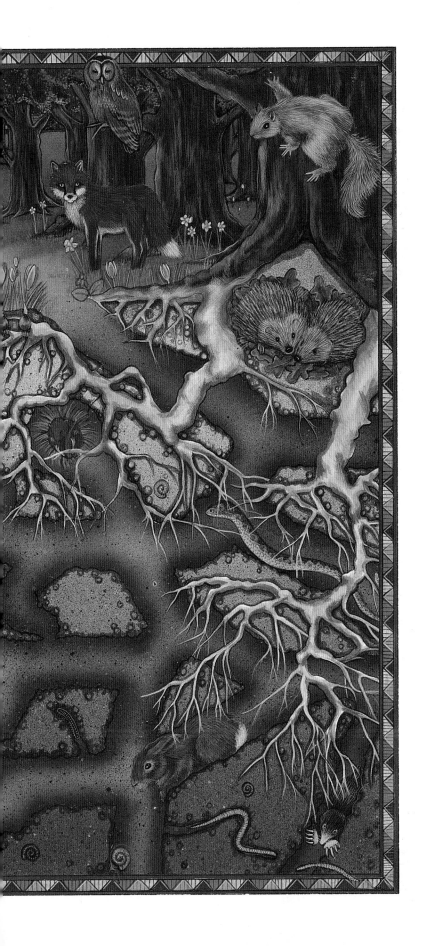

# LIFE UNDERGROUND

Beneath the ground, in a warm, snug nest, six baby rabbits lie sleeping. A short time before, their mother had left them to gather food in the woods.

Now, as the sun begins to set and the moon rises high in the sky, she makes her way back to the burrow.

But it is not a simple journey. Many dangers await her. Prowling creatures in search of food block the entrances. Tunnels have collapsed or are occupied by other animals — some hunting her and her babies. Can you find the way back to the nest? Follow the tunnels through the maze of the rabbit warren, but beware — only one path is clear and leads to home.

# PATHWAYS IN THE SNOW

Summer has come to the snowy wastes of the Arctic tundra. Flowers bloom, insects buzz, and the female lemmings and their pups enjoy the warm sunshine while they search for food along the water's edge. As daylight fades, the adult lemmings realize with alarm that they are far from home. They must get their pups back to the burrow, but the way is blocked by grazing animals, deep snowdrifts and hungry enemies hunting for their supper. The pups are too young to swim through the ice-cold water or cross the freezing marsh and snow. Instead, they must travel over the land. Can you help them? Find the way back to the lemmings' burrow, but remember — only one path leads safely home.

# TO THE SEA

In the early morning, just before sunrise, on a lonely beach in Costa Rica, hundreds of newly hatched green turtles scrabble from their underground nests to the surface of the sand. They begin to make their way to the sea. But their journey is not easy. Some are confused by the twinkling lights of a nearby village, mistaking them for the moon glinting on the sea. Others fall prey to raccoons and coatis. Gulls hover overhead, waiting to swoop, and other shore creatures block the way. Some turtles even fall into the deep ruts made by a beach buggy as it churned its way across the wet sand. Can you tell which turtles will make it safely to the sea? Follow their trails and find out.

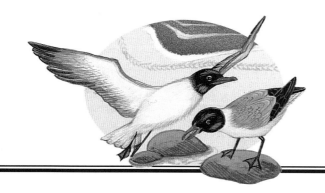

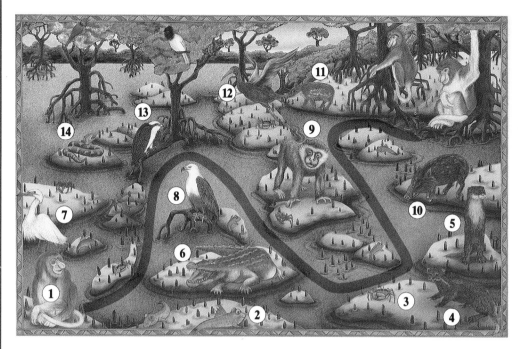

## SWAMPLANDS

*The mangrove swamps have once again been submerged by the incoming evening tide. A proboscis monkey must swim back to the jungle, but his path is blocked. The tangled roots of the mangrove trees sprout finger-like above the water, while the fearsome crocodile waits, jaws open, ready to pounce! Only one path is safe.*

**1. Proboscis monkey** Proboscis monkeys spend most of their time in the tree tops feeding on leaves, fruit and flowers. The male's long, bulbous nose straightens out when he makes his loud, honking call.

**2. Mudskipper** These strange little fish can climb, walk and skip over the mud. Their large mobile eyes help them to see well out of water, and they move by using their strong pectoral (shoulder) fins.

**3. Fiddler crab** The male fiddler crab has one small and one huge claw. Its small claw is used for feeding. Its large claw plays a dual role, used both as a weapon to warn off other males, and to wave invitingly to attract a passing female.

**4. Crab-eating mongoose** This mongoose hunts alone, usually at night, feeding on crabs and similar creatures. The mongoose marks the boundary of its den with a scent to warn away other animals.

**5. Eurasian otter** Now rare, Eurasian otters live in burrows, called holts, in the river bank. Good swimmers, they use their large, webbed hind feet and thick, muscular tails to propel them through the water. Their nostrils and ears can be closed when they are swimming.

**6. Salt-water crocodile** One of the largest and most dangerous of animals, the estuarine crocodile is hunted for its skin and is now protected in many areas. Able to live even in salt water, it rarely comes on land.

**7. Great egret** Like all herons, the egret hunts in water. It waits motionless until it sights its prey, which it then seizes in its strong, sharp beak.

**8. Sea eagle** Sometimes called fishing eagles, these large birds have rough surfaces on the underside of their toes to help them grasp their slippery prey.

**9. Crab-eating macaque** Mostly active during the day, these small, long-tailed monkeys live on the ground near water. They feed on crabs and other small animals.

**10. Bearded pig** These large pigs have white whiskers on their cheeks and large warts beneath their eyes. They feed on plants and fruit, often following groups of monkeys and picking up the food they drop.

**11. Lesser mouse deer** The smallest of the mouse deer or chevrotains, weighing only 2 kg, these shy creatures mainly come out at night. They do not have horns or antlers, but the males have long upper canine teeth that hang down below their jaws.

**12. Glossy ibis** The most widespread ibis, it feeds on insects and water creatures. The female nests in a tree or reed bed, and both parents care for the eggs and young.

**13. Osprey** At breeding time, the osprey, or fish hawk, builds a large nest on the ground from sticks and seaweed. The same nest is often used year after year until it becomes huge. The male feeds the female while she incubates the eggs and he also helps to feed the fledglings.

**14. Mangrove snake** A great many of these rear-fanged snakes live at the swamp's edge, feeding on crabs and fish.

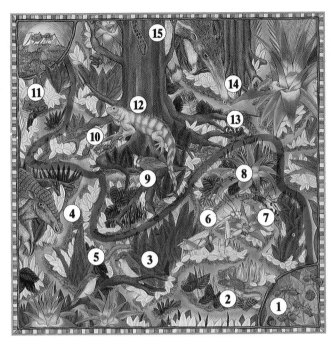

## A WORLD IN MINIATURE

*In the dense South American jungle, tiny leaf-cutter ants march back to their nests. But their way is blocked by many hazards, from hungry birds to the sticky-tongued anteater. Only one path leads safely to the nest.*

**1. Leaf-cutter ant** These tiny jungle insects cut off pieces of leaf with their sharp jaws and take them back to their nest. They carry the pieces, often larger than themselves, over their heads like enormous umbrellas. Because of this, they are also called parasol ants.

**2. Spiny pocket mouse** These tiny, bristly mice, sometimes called rice rats, usually come out at night to feed on seeds.

**3. Ochre-bellied flycatcher** This active little bird flits from tree to tree seizing insects and spiders in its hook-tipped bill.

**4. Giant armadillo** The largest armadillo, weighing up to 60 kg, this animal has an armoured body with movable horny plates.

It feeds on ants and termites, smashing their hills with its large-clawed front feet and flicking them up with its tongue.

**5. Tropical centipede** These fast-moving creatures have a pair of poison claws (modified front legs) just behind their head. This tropical species can grow up to 30 centimetres long.

**6. Praying mantis** Motionless, mantises sit hidden among the greenery, with their legs held as if in prayer, waiting to pounce on their unsuspecting prey.

**7. Long-horned beetle** The antennae of these beetles can be four times as long as their bodies. The grubs burrow into wood, weakening and spoiling it for building use.

**8. Arrow poison frog** The brilliant colours of these tiny ground-dwelling frogs warn their enemies that they are poisonous. Local tribespeople extract the poison and use it on the tips of their arrows and blow-pipe darts.

**9. Antbird** These tiny birds, most of them less than 10 centimetres long, have strong, hooked beaks. Many live on the dense forest floor in Central and South America, feeding on ants and other insects.

**10. Soldier termite** Termites differ from ants in that when the young hatch, they look like small adults, not grubs. The powerful jaws of some soldier termites can snap an ant in half.

**11. Horned frog** As broad as it is long, this large-mouthed frog spends much of its life half-buried in the ground.

**12. Common iguana** These agile tree-living lizards feed on plants, but they can defend themselves with sharp teeth and claws if attacked by predators.

**13. Caecilian** These strange limbless creatures look like giant earthworms but are in fact amphibians. Caecilians burrow into the soft soil of the forest floor in search of their prey of earthworms and insects and rarely appear above ground.

**14. Giant anteater** A giant anteater, walking on the knuckles of its front feet to protect its sharp claws, snuffles over the forest floor in search of food. Like the armadillo, it demolishes ant nests and termite mounds, then mops up the insects with its sticky tongue, which can extend up to 60 centimetres.

**15. Anaconda** One of the largest snakes at up to 12 metres long, the anaconda can climb small trees and shrubs but never strays far from water.

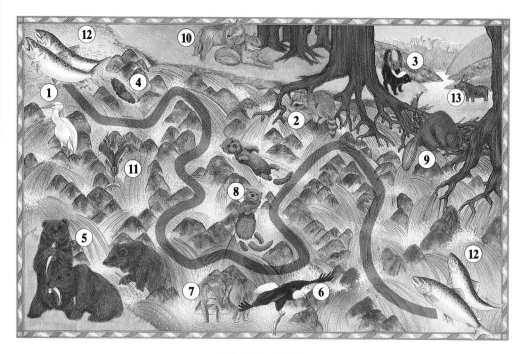

## UPSTREAM

*The salmon have swum hundreds of kilometres from the Atlantic Ocean to a river in North America. Their journey is almost at its end, but they still face many hazards, from hunting osprey to bears fishing with their cubs. Only one waterway will lead them safely to the spawning grounds, where the female will lay her eggs.*

**1. Great white egret** During the breeding season, these egrets develop long plumes of feathers on their back, and their bill turns from bright yellow to black.

**2. Common raccoon** With their fox-like faces, black eye-masks and ringed tails, raccoons are instantly recognizable. They usually hunt at night, feeding on frogs, crabs, fish, birds and eggs.

**3. Striped skunk** Most skunks warn away their enemies by stamping their feet, raising their tails and walking stiff-legged. If this fails, they will spray the intruder with a foul-smelling liquid.

**4. American mink** Close relatives of weasels and polecats, minks live in waterside dens. They see poorly under water, but their partly webbed feet help them to swim well. They are often bred in captivity for their fine fur coats.

**5. Grizzly bear** Grizzlies love water and are keen salmon fishers, catching the fish with their teeth or claws. The female teaches the cubs to hunt when they are a few months old. These huge beasts are now endangered in many areas due to hunting and loss of habitat.

**6. Bald eagle** The national symbol of the United States, bald eagles have a spectacular courtship ritual in which they lock talons in midair and turn somersaults.

Their nests, added to year after year, can be up to 2.5 metres deep and 3.5 metres wide.

**7. Coyote** Also known as prairie or brush wolves, coyotes live alone or in small packs. They keep in touch with each other using a wide range of calls, from their well-known howls to yelps, barks and wails.

**8. River otter** North American or Canadian river otters call to each other using short chuckles and chirps. They are keen hunters, feeding on frogs, crayfish, crabs and fish.

**9. Beaver** Members of the rodent family, beavers have stable family groups. The male and female form a long-term partnership and both parents care for the young, called kits or pups, for up to 2 years.

**10. Wolf** Pack members hunt together and will run down deer and caribou. Each wolf has a place in the order of the pack, which is maintained by gestures and postures. For example, the leader of the pack – the dominant male – carries his tail higher than the others.

**11. Osprey** Sometimes called the fish hawk, the osprey is a keen hunter. When it sights a fish, it plunges feet forward into the water and grasps its prey in both feet. Small spikes on the soles of its feet help it grip its slippery meal.

**12. Salmon** As salmon migrate upstream to lay their eggs, the lower jaws of the breeding males become hook-shaped. The eggs are laid in a redd, or heap of stones, formed by the female lashing her tail.

**13. Moose** The largest deer, the moose, or elk, has a broad drooping muzzle, a large flap of skin (the bell) hanging from its throat, and enormous branched antlers. The males have fierce mock fights, clashing and locking their antlers.

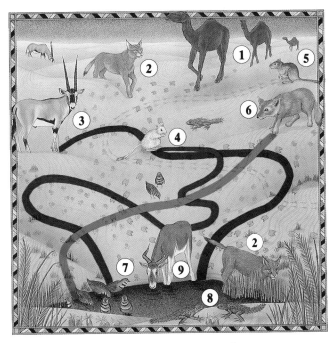

## DESERT WASTES

*As the sun goes down, many animals make their way to an oasis in the Sahara desert. Some animals have already arrived; others are on their way. Which ones make it to the cooling water?*

**1. Dromedary (one-humped) camel** The camel does not store water in its hump but in its stomach lining. It can go for days without water and lose up to 27 per cent of its body weight without being harmed. A camel can make up this loss in 10 minutes – one reportedly drank over 100 litres of water in a few minutes.

**2. Caracal** The caracal, or desert lynx, usually hunts at night. Caracals feed on young kudus and small antelopes as well as jerboas, hares, and various birds. They can leap up to 2 metres high and strike down a bird in midair.

**3. Scimitar oryx** These beautiful antelopes are hunted for their long, gracefully curving horns. Although they can go without water for several days, scimitar oryx usually

move south to slightly cooler areas in the dry season. They live in small groups and feed mainly on grass. They may look gentle, but the males are fierce fighters. The males and females have mock battles during courtship. They lower their heads and lock horns, pushing each other around in circles. The pair may spin round over 20 times.

**4. Desert jerboa** Desert jerboas live in deep underground burrows. They use their front teeth and short front legs to dig and their long hind feet to kick away the sand. Jerboas leap across the desert on their hind feet and use their tail as a balance. They do not drink water because they get all they need from the food they eat.

**5. North African gerbil** Living in groups of about 12, these gerbils hide by day in

simple burrows dug in the sand. They emerge at dusk to search for seeds and plants, jumping across the desert on their long back legs. Like jerboas, they get water from the food they eat, so they do not need to drink.

**6. Fennec fox** The smallest fox, the fennec measures 36–38 centimetres from nose to tail. Its huge ears, about 16 centimetres long, help it to keep cool. It shelters in burrows in the sand, emerging at night to feed on birds, insects and lizards.

**7. Spotted sandgrouse** The size of small pigeons, these beautifully marked birds have short legs with feathers extending down to the toes. Sandgrouse are strong fliers and flock to a water hole at the same time every day. Some sandgrouse lay their eggs in the footprints of large animals, such as camels; others nest in small depressions. Both the male and female birds incubate the eggs and bring the chicks food and water.

**8. Spiny agama** These lizards live in the dry desert areas of North Africa. Deserts are cold at night, and the lizards get so cold that they cannot move around much. However, as the sun heats the desert sand, the agamas warm up too and start moving and hunting again. They shelter under shrubs during the hottest part of the day. Spiny agamas usually chase and catch small insects, but they also eat grass, seeds and berries.

**9. Addax** These shy creatures, also called screwhorn antelopes, have long spiral horns up to a metre in length. The horns are so highly prized by hunters that addax are now rare in the wild, but they are being bred in many zoos. Addax can survive in the depths of the desert, where the only sources of water are the grass and seeds that they eat, but they will drink large amounts of water when it is available.

## ON THE RIVER

*The peace of the river is broken by the female beaver's alarm signal. Her mate has to find his way through the river maze and return to the dam. But he doesn't want to disturb the other animals and so must find a clear pathway to his lodge.*

**1. European beaver** Once hunted for their beautiful fur, European beavers are now quite rare. Like North American beavers, they build vast dams of felled trees, mud and stones which turn streams into pools.

**2. Kingfisher** The brilliant jewel-like colours of this bird shimmer as it dives below the water to seize fish in its sharp beak.

**3. Water shrew** These tiny creatures live in the river bank. Shrews mark their tunnels with scent from special glands on their backs to warn other animals to keep out.

**4. Otter** The webbed feet of these sleek animals help them to swim at up to 12 km an hour. Otters can stay under water for up to 4 minutes.

**5. Water vole** Often called water rats, these shaggy creatures paddle along using all four feet to swim.

**6. Pochard** A diving duck, the pochard builds its nest in a mound of reeds in which the hen lays up to 17 eggs.

**7. Natterjack toad** The male's loud mating call can be heard over 2 km away. These toads mate at night; the female lays strings of up to 4,000 eggs in the water. The eggs hatch into water-living tadpoles that slowly metamorphose, or change, into adults which live most of their lives on land.

**8. Mallard ducks** During courtship, the bright male and the duller female mallard preen each other's blue wing patches.

**9. Grey heron** Herons often wade into the water to search for fish, but they will also eat young birds, eggs, snakes and plants.

**10. Mute swan** One of the heaviest flying birds at up to 23 kg, these birds mate for life, both parents caring for the cygnets.

**11. Pike** The pike's mottled skin makes it difficult to see as it hides among the reeds. A ferocious hunter, it darts out to trap its unsuspecting prey of fish and birds.

**12. Common frog** Adult frogs live on land, returning to the water to mate. Unlike toads, frogs' eggs are laid in clumps – but they develop into adults in a similar way.

**13. Teal** These small ducks are usually found in flocks. Teal often fly in formation, turning and landing together.

**14. Emperor dragonfly** These large dragonflies have a 10-centimetre wingspan and a body almost 7 centimetres long.

**15. Shoveler duck** As the shoveler duck swims, it sucks water in through its flat, broad bill. As the water runs out, tiny plant and animal food is left behind.

**16. Great crested grebe** Before they mate, these grebe perform a complicated dance. They wag their heads, display their wings and give each other water weeds.

**17. Grass snake** An active hunter, the grass snake preys on frogs, toads and newts. Although it can kill small animals with its poison, it usually swallows its prey alive.

**18. Banded demoiselle** The pearly patches on this damselfly's wings make them look banded as it flutters among the flowers.

**19. Brown rat** Originally from Asia, brown rats are found wherever people live. They are serious pests and can carry disease.

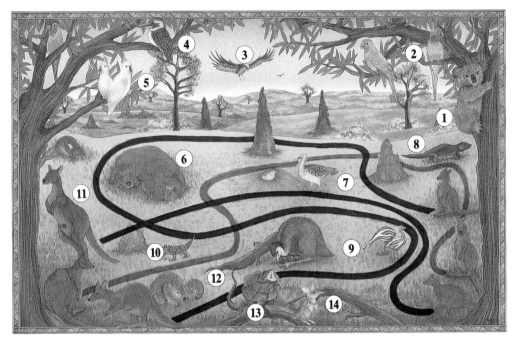

## THE OUTBACK

*The call of a dingo has frightened three baby kangaroos as they play in the Australian bush. They make their way back to the safety of their mothers' pouches. But which joey belongs to which kangaroo?*

**1. Koala** The tree-dwelling koala lives in dry forests on the edge of the bush. It feeds only on the leaves and shoots of a few species of eucalyptus, and an adult will eat over 1 kg of leaves a day.

**2. Princess parrot** Although a rare bird, this parrot can be found throughout the interior of Australia wherever there is scrubland. Rarely seen, this beautiful bird is now protected by law.

**3. Wedge-tailed eagle** Australia's mightiest bird, this eagle soars high in the sky ready to dive, talons outstretched, on unsuspecting rabbits and other small mammals.

**4. Kookaburra** The largest of the kingfishers, the kookaburra eats anything from insects to small mammals and birds.

Its noisy, laughing call breaks the silence at dawn and at dusk.

**5. Sulphur-crested cockatoo** Flocks of these noisy birds may number up to 100 in the open plains. Cockatoos fly to daytime feeding grounds and return to their roosting sites at night.

**6. Dingo** Descended from domestic dogs introduced by the Aborigines thousands of years ago, dingos usually feed on sheep and rabbits, although a pack will attack kangaroos, especially joeys.

**7. Mallee fowl** In winter, the male mallee digs a pit in the ground and fills it with dead plants. He covers this with sand, and as the plants rot they give off heat. The bird tests the temperature, keeping it about 33°C by

opening up the mound to cool it, or adding more sand to keep it warm. The female lays her eggs in holes in the mound, and the male looks after them until they hatch.

**8. Gould's goanna** Sometimes called the sand monitor, the large, 1.6-metre long goanna feeds on insects, birds, small mammals and reptiles.

**9. Emu** Emus are large, flightless birds. The male incubates the eggs, rarely leaving the nest for the 8 weeks it takes them to hatch. He cares for the chicks until they can look after themselves.

**10. Moloch** Also known as the thorny devil, this harmless lizard is covered with a mass of spikes on its body, tail and legs to protect it from its enemies. It feeds on ants, crushing their hard bodies with its flattened teeth.

**11. Red kangaroo** These majestic animals travel into the bush after the rains, when food is plentiful. They move on their back legs, bounding across the land at speeds of over 20 km an hour. The joeys, weighing less than 3/4 gram at birth, stay in the pouch for several months, often returning there when danger threatens.

**12. Hairy-nosed wombat** This scrubland animal digs burrows that stretch for over 13 metres underground. The female gives birth in the autumn, and the young wombat remains in the pouch for up to 3 months.

**13. Frilled lizard** When threatened, this spectacular reptile opens its mouth wide to unfold the large frill around its neck. It runs across the ground on two legs, hunting for insects and other small animals.

**14. Greater bilby** The soft, blue-grey bilbies, or rabbit-eared bandicoots, live in deep burrows underground. They emerge at night to feed on seeds, bulbs and insects.

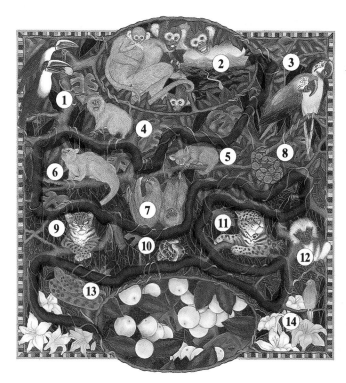

## IN THE JUNGLE

*Deep within the rain forest of South America, a troupe of squirrel monkeys is climbing through the tree tops. Below them they spy the juicy, golden fruits of the guava tree. But how can they reach the fruit without disturbing the other creatures of the forest?*

**1. Toucan** The toucan's bill is huge but light because its bony tissue is filled with air bubbles. Toucans pick up fruit with their long bills. Then, with a flick of the head, they toss the fruit into their mouths.

**2. Squirrel monkey** These agile monkeys use their long, prehensile (grasping) tails to grip the branches as they travel through the rain forest. Newborn babies hitch a ride on their mother's back.

**3. Macaw** These brilliantly coloured birds, members of the parrot family, live in noisy, screeching flocks. They feed on fruits, nuts and seeds – their strong beaks can even crack the hard shells of Brazil nuts!

**4, 12. Tamarin** These silky-soft monkeys have distinct tufts or manes of fur. Instead of grasping branches or swinging through the trees like most monkeys, tamarins use their clawed fingers and toes for balance and run along the branches like squirrels.

**5. Opossum** Opossums are marsupials – their young develop in a pouch. The woolly opossum has large eyes and good eyesight. It feeds on fruit and nectar, and is an agile climber, using its prehensile tail, as well as its hands and feet, to grasp branches.

**6. Kinkajou** The kinkajou has thick, short fur and a long, prehensile tail. Although kinkajous usually feed on fruit, they also use their long, mobile tongues to lick up nectar and honey.

**7. Sloth** Sloths are renowned for their extraordinarily slow movements. They feed on leaves and spend much of their lives motionless, hanging upside down. The greenish colour of their fur, which comes from the tiny plants that live on the sloths, camouflages them in the leafy tree tops.

**8. Boa constrictor** Although it usually lives on the ground, the boa constrictor can climb trees by grasping the branches with its tail. It kills birds and small mammals by crushing or suffocating them within the coils of its body.

**9. Ocelot** The ocelot, prized for its beautiful coat, is one of the many small cats threatened with extinction. It usually hunts at night for small mammals, birds and reptiles. During the day it sleeps, safely hidden among the foliage.

**10. Tree boa** The brilliant green boa is well camouflaged among the leaves as it waits coiled around a branch. From here, it can easily seize and kill birds, bats and other unsuspecting prey with its sharp teeth.

**11. Jaguar** The largest cat of the New World, the jaguar is a powerful hunter. It usually hunts on the ground, but it is an excellent climber and will pursue its prey of monkeys and birds through the trees.

**13. Anaconda** Anacondas usually live in swampy fresh water, but they can climb small trees. They often lie in wait for their prey, striking quickly to envelop it in their coils and drag it into the water.

**14. Parakeet** These noisy forest dwellers climb among the trees using their hooked beaks as well as their feet. Before they start to feed, parakeets often taste the fruit or seeds with their fleshy tongue.

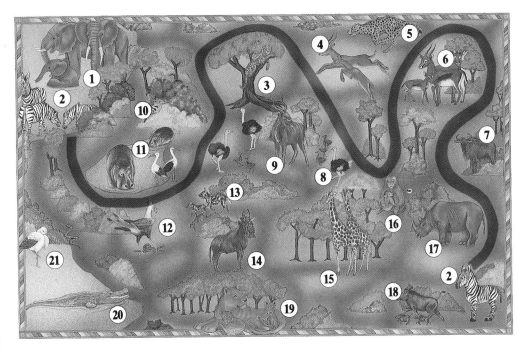

## AT THE WATER HOLE

*It is just after sunrise and many animals are making their way to the water hole. A young zebra has become separated from the rest of the herd. It tries to get back to its mother, but there is only one safe route to take.*

**1. African elephant** An elephant's flexible trunk, actually an elongated nose and upper lip, is used for gathering food, drinking, smelling and even for fighting.

**2. Burchell's zebra** Zebras live in herds and are active by day. They recognize each other by their stripe patterns as well as by sound and scent. Burchell's is the most common zebra in Africa.

**3. Leopard** The leopard's beautiful spotted coat hides it as it prowls through the trees and sleeps among leafy branches.

**4. Impala** This fleet-footed antelope can leap as high as 3 metres and as far as 10 metres. Male impalas have long lyre-shaped horns; the females are hornless.

**5. Cheetah** The fastest land animal, this graceful cat can reach speeds up to 96 km an hour over short distances.

**6. Thomson's gazelle** Small and graceful, these gazelle are easily recognized by the dark stripes along their sides.

**7. Black wildebeest** Herds of black wildebeest migrate up to 1,000 km in search of food and water.

**8. Ostrich** Too big to fly, the ostrich is the fastest creature on two legs, running at up to 70 km an hour.

**9. Greater kudu** Female kudus are usually hornless; the males have long spiralled horns.

**10. Hoopoe** A ground-dwelling bird, the hoopoe usually holds its huge crest flat, raising it only when alarmed or courting.

**11. Hippo** Hippos wallow in mud to keep cool. They can even walk under water.

**12. Secretary bird** This long-legged bird may walk up to 80 km a day in search of its prey of insects, snakes and small rodents.

**13. African wild dog** Packs of hunting dogs roam over a wide area looking for prey. They work together to kill large animals such as antelope and wildebeest.

**14. Topi** The most numerous of African antelopes, topis can go without water for up to 30 days.

**15. Giraffe** The giraffe's long neck allows it to reach the highest leaves, but when it drinks, it has to spread its front legs wide and bend its knees to reach the water.

**16. Hamadryas baboon** The male baboon, twice the size of the female, has a heavy mane on his head and shoulders.

**17. Black rhinoceros** Rhinos often wallow in mud to keep cool. The mobile upper lip is used for grasping leaves and twigs.

**18. Warthog** Although the upper tusks are larger, the warthog uses its small, sharp lower tusks in fighting.

**19. Lion** The females of a pride (group) of lions do most of the hunting, killing their prey with a bite to the neck.

**20. Nile crocodile** After seizing its prey, the crocodile holds it under water to drown it.

**21. White stork** These storks nest in Europe, then migrate south to spend the winter in Africa.

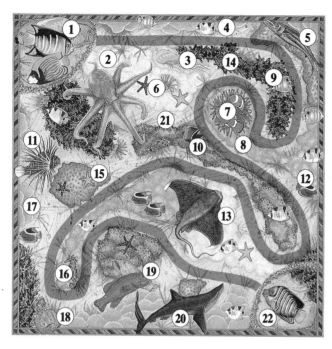

## ON THE REEF

*The waters of Australia's Great Barrier Reef are home to thousands of amazing and beautiful sea creatures. Here a jewel-like banded angelfish is trying to return to its shelter near the other angelfish, but in the way are hungry enemies and other creatures of the reef.*

**1, 22. Angelfish; 4, 10, 12. Butterflyfish** Each kind of angelfish and butterflyfish has a special pattern of bright colours. Scientist Konrad Lorenz discovered that these colours act as a warning, telling other fish to keep out of their territories.

**2. Common octopus** Hiding among the rocks and corals, the octopus uses its eight long arms with their powerful suckers to defend itself against its enemies and pull its prey into its fearful beaked jaws.

**3. Portuguese man-of-war** As the wind catches its large air-filled float, this colourful jellyfish is swept across the water's surface. Beneath the waves trails a mass of beautiful but poisonous tentacles, which trap unsuspecting prey.

**5. Barracuda** Fast-moving adult barracudas, with their needle-sharp teeth, are fearsome predators. They swim in shoals (groups), attacking fish and other sea creatures.

**6, 15. Starfish** These colourful starfish move across the reef using hundreds of tiny sucker-like tube feet on the underside of their five arms.

**7. Clownfish; 8. Sea anemone** Hidden safely among the anemone's stinging tentacles lives the clownfish. The anemone protects the clownfish from its enemies, and in return the clownfish chases away other fish that feed on the anemone's soft tentacles.

**9. Beaked coralfish** The bright stripes of the coralfish confuse its enemies by breaking up its outline and disguising its eye. A large, bright eyespot near its tail adds to the confusion, making would-be predators think that its tail is its head.

**11. Lionfish** The lionfish's amazing array of fins and stripes helps to camouflage it. At night it emerges to hunt, killing small fish with its poisonous spines.

**13. Eagle ray** As it moves across the reef, the eagle ray feeds on shellfish, crushing them with its powerful teeth. It defends itself by lashing its enemies with its tail, which is armed with a poison spine.

**14, 17, 21. Coral** Despite their rock-like appearance, coral reefs are formed from the limestone skeletons of millions of tiny animals. The living corals are small animals called polyps. They have a mouth at the top surrounded by stinging tentacles, which they spread out to catch food.

**16. Sea horse** The armoured sea horse is most unusual: in the breeding season the female lays her eggs in the brood pouch of the male fish. After 4 to 5 weeks the male "gives birth" to perfect tiny sea horses.

**18. Stonefish** The stonefish lies half-buried waiting to ambush its unsuspecting prey. Its needle-sharp poison spines protect it from its enemies and kill the fish on which it feeds.

**19. Grouper** The strong jaws of these large fish are armed with sharp, backward-pointing teeth. Groupers snap up any animal that ventures into their territory, and they can change their colour to match the corals in which they hide.

**20. Blue shark** These fast-swimming streamlined predators search for prey among the corals. They will attack most animals, from small fish to other sharks and octopus.

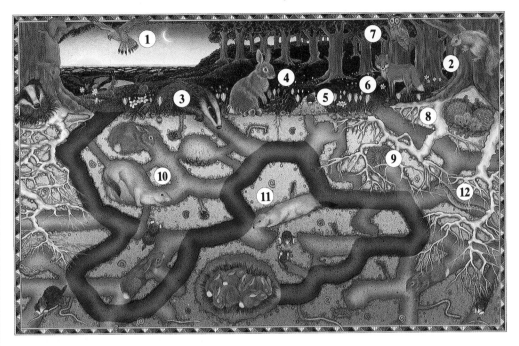

## LIFE UNDERGROUND

*In this European woodland clearing at twilight, many nocturnal (active at night) animals have emerged to search for food. The mother rabbit has to find the route through the maze back to her nest. But the weasel, fox and other predators — as well as their intended prey — are barring her way.*

**1. Kestrel** A common bird of prey in Europe, the kestrel is a master of hovering flight. It hangs almost motionless in the air, searching the ground below for the slightest movement. Then it swoops, catching its unsuspecting prey in its sharp talons.

**2. Squirrel** Relatives of rats, red and grey squirrels are agile climbers and spend much of their lives in the trees. They build dome-shaped nests, called dreys, out of twigs, and line them with moss and grass.

**3. Badger** A member of the weasel family, the badger is easily recognized by its distinctive black and white striped face. Groups of up to twelve live together in a large underground network of tunnels called a sett. The badger has very poor eyesight but an excellent sense of smell. It usually feeds on plants, earthworms and other small creatures, but it will dig out and eat young rabbits if it finds them.

**4. Rabbit** This furry mammal lives in family groups in a vast network of underground tunnels or burrows called a warren. The female rabbits, called does, rear their young in the central part of the warren in nests lined with fur and dried grass.

**5. Mole** The enormous front feet of the velvety-coated mole are ideally suited for digging through soil. Moles spend most of their life underground. Excellent hunters of earthworms and other similar creatures, they eat about half their own body weight in food each day.

**6. Fox** Well known for their beautiful long, bushy tails, or brushes, foxes are most active at dusk and at night. Solitary hunters, they will eat almost anything, but they prefer young rabbits and rodents. Their young, called cubs, are born in early spring in well-hidden dens.

**7. Tawny owl** One of the most common owls in Europe, the tawny owl's ghostly call of "to-whit, to-whoo-oo" breaks the silence of the night in early spring. Sharp eyesight and hearing help the owl hunt its prey even on the darkest night.

**8. Hedgehog** The hedgehog hibernates (sleeps) in winter, emerging in the spring to feed on worms, slugs, beetles and snails. When in danger, a hedgehog rolls itself up into a tight ball.

**9. Dormouse** So called because in the winter it is dormant, or hibernates, the dormouse lives in European woods. It wraps its tail around its head and, except for an occasional meal from its store of nuts, stays in its nest until spring.

**10. Stoat** In cold winters the stoat grows a white coat and is called an ermine. In the spring it moults (sheds its fur) and grows red-brown fur on its back with a creamy-white belly and a black tip on its long tail. It feeds on small mammals such as rabbits, which are often paralysed by fear at the sight of it and make no attempt to escape.

**11. Weasel** Unlike the stoat, the weasel keeps its red-brown coat all year and has a short tail. Small enough to chase its prey deep into the burrow, it usually eats rats and mice, but it will also kill young rabbits.

**12. Adder** The broad black zigzag line along its back and the black spots on its sides identify the poisonous adder, or European viper. Just one bite paralyses the small animals on which the adder feeds.

## PATHWAYS IN THE SNOW

*As the summer sun warms the frozen Arctic tundra, the snow melts and for a brief time flowers bloom and animal life abounds. As daylight fades, the female lemmings and their pups must return to their burrow. But only one path leads to home.*

**1. Caribou** These North American reindeer travel over 1,000 km twice a year between their summer and winter feeding grounds. Their habit of digging through the snow to find food led the Micmac Indians to call them *caribou*, meaning "shoveler".

**2. Arctic wolf** Fierce hunters, a pack of Arctic wolves may travel over 1,000 km as they hunt caribou. Their ghostly howls keep them in touch with one another and warn other packs to keep away.

**3. Pomarine skua** These summer visitors breed on the tundra, feeding on lemmings. Skuas lay up to three brown eggs, which hatch into mottled honey-brown chicks.

**4. Ringed seal** In the winter, when ice covers the seas, ringed seals use the long sharp claws on their front flippers to cut holes in the ice. After diving to hunt fish, the seals surface at these holes to breathe.

**5. Snowy owl** Daytime hunters, snowy owls feed on Arctic hares and lemmings. They nest in May in small hollows lined with moss and feathers. The male feeds the female while she incubates the eggs.

**6. Musk ox** Their long, shaggy coats and dense underfur keep musk ox warm in the freezing Arctic winter. When threatened, they form a tight circle, with their heads and horns pointing at the enemy.

**7. Arctic fox** In its smoky grey summer coat, the Arctic fox blends in with its background. Its short ears and muzzle and furry-soled feet help to keep it warm in the freezing snow, and its snow-white winter coat conceals it from its enemies and its prey.

**8. Canada goose** When Canada geese migrate to their breeding and summer feeding grounds, these large birds always follow the same route and often breed in the same area where they were born.

**9. Arctic hare** Easy to recognize with their long, black-tipped ears and long hind legs, Arctic hares usually live alone. They rest in small burrows in the ground or in shallow depressions called forms. In the winter they grow a white coat.

**10. Polar bear** Excellent swimmers with "webbed" toes, polar bears spend most of their lives hunting seals among the ice floes. In summer, they journey across the land, feeding on lemmings and plants.

**11. Trumpeter swan** These beautiful birds breed on the tundra, laying their eggs in a nest of grass and moss lined with swan's down. When the cygnets are less than 90 days old, trumpeter swans journey south to overwinter in a warmer climate.

**12. Walrus** The walrus uses its snout and tusks (long canine teeth) to pry shellfish from the ocean floor. The food is then gathered into the mouth by the mobile lips.

**13. Lemming** These little animals are active even in winter, feeding on the seeds and plants they find in their snow tunnels. Lemmings usually have two litters a year. At times the number of animals increases so enormously that they have to find new places to live. They often swim across lakes and rivers and may even try to swim the sea.

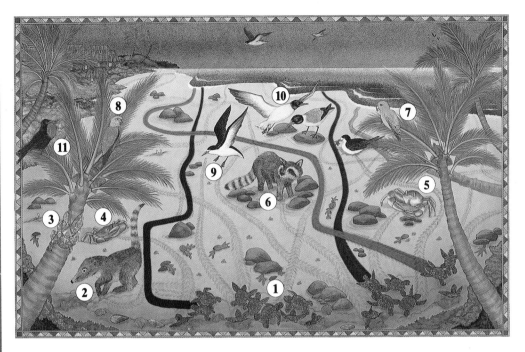

## TO THE SEA

*As the newly hatched green turtles make their way to the sea, they are confronted by many dangers — raccoons, coatis and gulls, which will eat them, and the twinkling lights of a nearby town, which confuse them. Only a few of the hatchlings will reach the safety of the sea.*

**1. Green turtle** At nesting time, green turtles travel hundreds of kilometres to lay their eggs on the beaches where they were born. The female makes a hollow in the sand with her front flippers. Lying in this hollow, so that her shell is level with the sand, she digs a deep hole with her hind flippers and lays over 100 eggs. She covers the nest with sand and returns to the sea. The eggs hatch 2 to 3 months later. The hatchlings dig their way out and head for the sea. Many die. The green turtle is now an endangered species because it has been hunted for its eggs, hide and meat, and is losing its habitat along the beach.

**2. Coati** Although they usually live in woods and lowland forests, coatis will venture on to beaches to hunt for food.

The coati snuffles in the ground with its long, mobile snout, feeding on insects, spiders and small animals. It will also dig up and eat turtle eggs as well as the young hatchlings.

**3. Robber crab** The robber crab weighs up to 2 kg and is half a metre long. It climbs trees, feeding on fruit and coconuts.

**4. Land crab** Square-bodied land crabs feed on both plants and animals. They live mainly on land, only occasionally returning to the sea.

**5. Ghost crab** This sand crab lies in burrows beneath the sand with just its long eye stalks visible. The ghost crab usually feeds on sand flies but also attacks newly

hatched turtles, catching them by a flipper and dragging them underground.

**6. Raccoon** The raccoon hunts at night, using its front paws and long fingers to handle its food. It climbs well and can also swim. Although it usually lives in woods and swamps near water, it will also forage on beaches, digging up turtle eggs and hunting for hatchlings.

**7. Spectacled parrotlet** Found throughout Central America, these small parrots live in noisy, chattering flocks of between 5 and 20 birds. They live in open forest, feeding on berries, buds, blossoms and fruit.

**8. Yellow-headed parrot** Good talkers, these bright, colourful parrots are under threat because they are collected in large numbers for the cage-bird trade. They are also in danger from the destruction of their forest homes.

**9. Black skimmer** Skimmers have a special way of catching fish. They fly just above the surface of the sea so that their flattened lower bill cuts through the water. When a skimmer comes upon a fish or crab, it snaps its upper bill closed, pulls it head sharply back to swallow its prey, and keeps on flying. In spring, when skimmers breed, the female scrapes out a hollow in the sand in which she lays 2 to 4 eggs.

**10. Black-headed gull** These small, active gulls feed on almost anything. Their black heads are part of their breeding plumage. Colonies of gulls nest on marshes and coasts in the spring.

**11. Magnificent frigate bird** This beautiful bird catches its prey of fish, crabs and, on this occasion, baby turtles by swooping down on them. The male has a large, red throat pouch which he blows up like a football to attract females.